For Cassidy May, with love
—M. R.

To my sister, Lucy
—S. M.

THIS IS A BORZOI BOOK PUBLISHED BY ALFRED A. KNOPF

Text copyright © 2009 by Mara Rockliff
Illustrations copyright © 2009 by Sarah McMenemy

Published in the United States by Alfred A. Knopf, an imprint of Random House Children's Books, a division of Random House, Inc., New York.

Knopf, Borzoi Books, and the colophon are registered trademarks of Random House, Inc.

Visit us on the Web! www.randomhouse.com/kids

Educators and librarians, for a variety of teaching tools, visit us at www.randomhouse.com/teachers

Library of Congress Cataloging-in-Publication Data
Rockliff, Mara.
The busiest street in town / written by Mara Rockliff ; illustrated by Sarah McMenemy. — 1st ed.
p. cm.
Summary: Best friends Agatha May Walker and Eulalie Scruggs, who live on opposite sides of busy Rushmore Boulevard, inspire their neighbors to
come together and make their street a much more pleasant place.
ISBN 978-0-375-84020-3 (trade) — ISBN 978-0-375-94020-0 (lib. bdg.)
[1. Roads—Fiction. 2. Traffic congestion—Fiction. 3. Neighborhood—Fiction.] I. McMenemy, Sarah, ill. II. Title.
PZ7.R5887Bus 2009
[Fic]—dc22
2008035884

The illustrations in this book were created using mixed media.

MANUFACTURED IN CHINA
October 2009
10 9 8 7 6 5 4 3 2 1
First Edition

THE BUSIEST STREET IN TOWN

Written by **Mara Rockliff** • Illustrated by **Sarah McMenemy**

Alfred A. Knopf  New York

Rushmore Boulevard was the busiest street in the entire town.

Cars *zipped* by this way and that way. Motorcycles **roared** by on their way from here to there. Giant trucks **rumbled** and **grumbled**, coming through, coming through.

Agatha May Walker lived on
Rushmore Boulevard.

Her dear friend *Eulalie Scruggs* lived on the other side.

One day, **Agatha** decided to go see **Eulalie**. She baked up a batch of sweet and spicy gingersnaps, and then she put on her best hat and headed out the door.

Cars *zipped* by. Motorcycles **roared**. Giant trucks **rumbled** and **grumbled**, coming through, coming through.

BEEP BEEP

SLOW DOWN

"Slow down!" said *Agatha*. "Slow down!"

They didn't.

Agatha went back inside.

When **Eulalie Scruggs** looked out a little later,
she saw something she had never seen before on
Rushmore Boulevard.

A wingback chair was sitting smack-dab in the middle of the street, and her friend *Agatha* was sitting in the chair.

"*Agatha May Walker!*" cried *Eulalie Scruggs*. "What in the world are you doing?" But the traffic was **too loud.**

Car horns **blasted**. Motorcycles **blared**. From a giant truck, a head poked out and bawled, "Out of the way! Coming through! Coming through!"

"Gingersnap?" *Agatha* offered. But the only answer was a giant cloud of smelly smoke.

Then **Eulalie** came out of her house. She had on her best hat, too, and she was lugging a piano stool, a card table, and a Parcheesi set.

"Parcheesi?"
said **Eulalie**.

"Don't mind if I do,"
said **Agatha**.

Cars slowed to a creep. Motorcycles crawled. A giant truck stopped, and the driver leaned way out to watch the game. "Can I play, too?" he asked.

With traffic slowing, people started to appear.

Mr. Solomon from down the street stopped with his poodle, Pearl, to try a sweet and spicy gingersnap. "Splendid!" he said, and traded *Agatha* his secret recipe for zesty lemon bars.

When the Rosado twins came home from school, they brought out colored chalk to draw a hopscotch board. Maggie, Madeline, and Mary Beth got out their jump rope and played Teddy Bear and Lemon Lime. And Crash-Test Chris, the Skateboard King, showed everybody how to do a nose grab and a big spin flip.

Something new was happening on Rushmore Boulevard.

Willie Spark borrowed the colored chalk and drew a picture of **Eulalie's** hat. He drew a fire-breathing dragon and then a fried egg. He drew a pirate, and a seashell, and a spaceship, and a foot. He even drew a big, deep hole that looked so real, none of the cars would drive over it, for fear of falling in.

Mrs. Mooney planted flowers all along the street. Sweet-smelling honeysuckle. Bright red poppies. Black-eyed Susans. Bluebells. Tulips. Tiger lilies. Giant yellow sunflowers that grew as high as trucks.

For their birthday, the Rosado twins had a huge, noisy, happy party on the street, with double the balloons. Everyone danced. The mariachi music was so popular, the band kept coming back.

Now there weren't so many cars and trucks and motorcycles as there used to be. But there were people. Children playing games. Teenagers playing music. People of all ages on their way from there to here.

And, in the middle of it all, *Agatha May Walker* in her wingback chair.

It took a while these days to drive down Rushmore Boulevard. But no one minded. If you drove too fast, you couldn't smell the honeysuckle. You wouldn't hear the music of the mariachi band. Worst of all, you'd miss the chance to sample one of **Agatha May Walker's** sweet and spicy gingersnaps.

One day when **Agatha** went out, she saw a brand-new street sign on the corner.

The busiest street in the entire town
was *Walker Road*.